D0121766

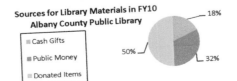

DANGER
&
DIAMONDS

DANGER & DIAMONDS

A MYSTERY at SEA

ELIZABETH LEVY

ILLUSTRATED BY **MORDICAI GERSTEIN**

ROARING BROOK PRESS

NEW YORK

Text copyright © 2010 by Elizabeth Levy
Illustrations copyright © 2010 by Mordicai Gerstein
Published by Roaring Brook Press
Roaring Brook Press is a division of Holtzbrinck Publishing Holdings
Limited Partnership
175 Fifth Avenue, New York, New York 10010
www.roaringbrookpress.com

Distributed in Canada by H. B. Fenn and Company Ltd.

Library of Congress Cataloging-in-Publication Data

Levy, Elizabeth, 1942–
    Danger and diamonds : a mystery at sea / Elizabeth Levy ; illustrated by
Mordicai Gerstein.—1st ed.
      p. cm.
    Summary: Eleven-year-old Philippa Bath, who loves mysteries, lives aboard a cruise
ship where her parents are employees, and when the new captain and his son arrive,
along with some royal guests, she is sure that something is wrong.
    ISBN 978-1-59643-462-2
    [1. Mystery and detective stories.   2. Cruise ships—Fictions.]   I. Gerstein,
Mordicai, ill.   II. Title.
PZ7.L5827Daj 2010
[Fic]—dc22   2010008183

Roaring Brook Press books are available for special promotions
and premiums.
For details contact: Director of Special Markets, Holtzbrinck Publishers.

First Edition October 2010
Book design by Scott Myles
Printed in September 2010 in the United States of America
by RR Donnelley & Sons Company, Harrisonburg, Virginia

1   3   5   7   9   8   6   4   2

To Marshall, a real diamond
in the rough. —E. L.

For Jill, Gwen, Fletcher,
and especially, Liz. —M. G.

TABLE OF CONTENTS

Danger
&
Diamonds

CHAPTER ONE

"DANGER!" SQUAWKED THE PARROT

I stared down at the dock from the deck of my ship. Okay, most eleven-year-olds don't get to call one of the world's great cruise ships, *theirs*. And no, I'm not rich; I don't own it. But I grew up on it! My parents have worked on the S.S. *Excalibur* for the last four years, and so I get to live on board the ship when we're out at sea. This is always my favorite time—right before a voyage begins. It must be like being backstage before a big rock show. Most of the crew is scurrying around getting ready for the guests, and every cruise has a different cast of characters coming on board. You never know what will happen!

A black Hummer SUV rolled up to the edge of the pier. The barricades that were usually there had been moved for the car. I wondered who warranted the VIP treatment. A boy about my age hopped out of the back of the SUV and opened the hatch. A long-legged white poodle bounded out of the car. The poodle looked around alertly, smelling the air. He had on a dog collar studded with huge rhinestones that gleamed in the sun. The dog stood calmly while the boy put a leash on him.

My father came up to me and leaned against the rail. My father has a swimmer's body, with a long torso and strong arms. He teaches water sports on board, and he says that almost from the moment I was born I loved the water as much as he did.

"That must be the new captain and his son," said Dad. I looked at the boy and his dog. The captain's son would, of course, have privileges the rest of us wouldn't dream of. I love animals and have always wanted one, but I'm not allowed to have any on the ship.

Mom came over and stood next to me. "Did you

know the captain's son is named Philip?" she asked. "Isn't that a strange coincidence? You're the same age, and you have almost the same name."

I fingered the little golden sea horse around my neck. Mom and Dad gave it to me when I was five. My name is Philippa. I love my first name. *Philippa* means lover of horses, and since I love both horses and the sea, the sea horse is my mascot.

"Does his name mean lover of horses, too?" I asked Mom.

She nodded.

"I wonder if the captain's son is going to think it a good coincidence or a bad one that our names sound the same?" I asked. Mom and Dad laughed as if I was making a joke. I wasn't. If the captain's son didn't like me, it would be a very long journey.

The son of the new captain reached into the backseat of the car and pulled out a big birdcage with a brightly colored parrot inside—*two* pets—now I was really jealous.

A man unfolded himself from the driver's side of the Hummer. He must have been over six feet five.

He was already wearing the white uniform of the captain.

The senior crewmembers were on the dock, standing in a straight line leading to the gangway. They snapped to attention as the boy and the captain came aboard. Our old captain, Captain Raynor, shook the new captain's hand. I wondered if it were hard to hand over his command. He said that once he retired he missed the sea every day. For this voyage, Captain Raynor signed on to be the tutor for the kids whose parents work on board and to give lectures for the passengers on the mysteries at sea. Captain Raynor didn't have any children and I am one of his favorites.

The boy and his dog looked like they couldn't wait to get aboard. The dog strained on his leash as they came up the gangway. My parents and I, and all the people who worked on the ship in activities and entertainment, stood up a little straighter to meet the captain and his son . . . and his pets!

"Ah, Captain Vittiganen," trilled Camilla Trout, our cruise director, "what a pleasure it is to have you and your son aboard. I want your son to meet my precious jewels, Ruby and Sapphire." Ruby and Sapphire are only nine—two years younger than I am, but just because their mother is my parents' boss, they think they are the boss of me. I wondered if the captain's son would be bossy, too. He couldn't be any worse than the Trout twins.

"I like your dog's collar," said Ruby. "They look like diamonds."

"Diamonds," repeated Sapphire. "Jewels, just like us."

"Danger!" squawked the bird in the cage.

"Did your bird just say *danger*?" I asked Philip.

"I think he said *diamonds*," said Ruby.

"Diamonds," repeated Sapphire.

"I heard *danger*," I said suspiciously.

"Philippa likes to make a big mystery out of everything!" Ruby whispered to Philip. "It gets so boring!"

"So boring!" repeated Sapphire.

"So is repeating everything your sister says," I snapped. I wished I could have bitten my tongue. I just can't control myself around the Trout girls, but I didn't want Philip to think that I was as mean as they are.

"Sorry," I muttered, "but there's nothing wrong with loving mysteries."

"I like mysteries, too," said Philip. "At least in books."

"I LOVE mysteries!" I said. "And I'm good at solving them. I love to find one to solve on each voyage." I held out my hand. To my astonishment, Philip's dog beat him to it and raised his paw. The dog was so tall that his paw reached my waist.

"My dog seems to like you," said Philip.

"What's his name?" I asked.

"Maximillian of Borgunlund," said Philip. It was quite a mouthful of a name for a dog.

"Hello, Max," I said, rubbing the dog under his chin. "I'm Philippa Bath." Max opened his big mouth into a doggy smile. I rubbed his ears. "Your dog is very beautiful."

Max's big doggy grin got even bigger.

Philip laughed. "My dog loves compliments. Poodles are very smart. They know when you're talking about them. The poodles of Borgunlund are famous."

"Borgunlund ... I've never heard of it," said Ruby.

"I have to admit, I haven't, either," I confessed.

Mom and Dad and I had sailed all over the world, and I had never heard of Borgunlund.

"It's between Finland and Russia," said Philip. "Not too many people have heard of my country."

"Borgunlund," I repeated. "It has a beautiful sound to it." The poodle looked up at me with his dark eyes.

Philip's eyes lit up. His dark eyes seemed to match his poodle's.

"Borgunlund *is* beautiful," he said. "We are on just a sliver of the North Sea. I was only a little boy when my family had to move."

"Maybe I'll ask Captain Raynor if we can study Borgunlund," I said to Philip.

Philip's expression cooled. "I don't think that's a good idea," he said. He sounded as if he were giving me an order.

Suddenly the parrot began to squawk. "Kiem *say*!! Kiem *say*!!"

I looked at Philip. "What is your parrot saying?" I asked.

"Oh, just nonsense," said Philip. I could swear the parrot's beady eyes looked right at me. As Philip walked away, his dog looked back at me, too—it was as if both animals wanted to warn me about something. Maybe the Trout twins were right. Maybe I liked mysteries just a little bit too much.

CHAPTER TWO

I AM A DUCHESS!

We were setting sail for San Aurelia, an island that the cruise line owns. It's one of the prettiest places in the world, with huge sandy beaches and wild horses that live on the beach grass. And nobody can go there unless they come with us, on the S.S. *Excalibur,* the biggest and most beautiful ship that sails the seas.

Every time we set sail, the ship's loudspeakers play "Anchors Aweigh." It's corny, but I still love it—to me the song signals the sound of adventure. No matter how many times I've done it, I get excited as I watch each new group of passengers come on board.

The crew guided the passengers into the main hall that we call the Royal Promenade. The captain was wearing his formal uniform, a white jacket with gold epaulets, indicating his rank. Phillip stood beside him in a suit. Everyone on the staff was spiffed up, including me. We were ready to do the meet and greet. My mother was sitting at a long table helping to check in the guests.

Waiters offered the adults champagne and the children fruit juices or ginger ale. Camilla went over to my mother, ready to double-check the room assignments. "Now, Meagan," Camilla said to Mom, "I want you to pay particular attention to the DeVaugn family. They are here for a family reunion. And they are very important."

"I treat all the passengers as if they are important," said Mom. "After all, they are."

"Well said," agreed Captain Vittiganen.

"Well, of course," said Camilla. My mother winked at me. Mom's main responsibility is ballroom-dance demonstrations and lessons, but like most people under Camilla, Mom has to do many jobs, especially on embarkation day. Mom and I both knew that Camilla was agreeing with her only because the captain was there. We don't have an official first class anymore, but the passengers who pay for the suites and the balcony rooms on the upper decks get extra service. And Camilla Trout has always treated the rich passengers way better than everyone else.

Just then, a very tall woman wearing wide purple pants and a bright red blouse with long, flowing sleeves swept past the others in line. Two teenage boys followed her. Neither of them looked very happy to be on board. "I am Marie DeVaugn," said the woman in a loud voice. "My nephews and I would like to be taken to our suite now."

"Hello and welcome. I will take you in a moment," said Mom. She smiled at the other passengers who had been standing in line patiently, unlike Ms. DeVaugn.

"Perhaps you didn't hear me," said Marie DeVaugn. "My family and I have booked the Royal Suite." She grinned a very toothy smile.

Her nephews looked miserable. I couldn't blame them. I'd be miserable, too, if that pushy lady was my aunt. I went up to them with two glasses of ginger ale that had been poured into champagne glasses. "Hi," I said. "I'm Philippa Bath. My parents work on board. Welcome!"

One of the boys snorted and poked his brother with his elbow. "Did you hear that, Arthur? 'Fill up a bath!'"

"Good one, Evan," said Arthur. He snorted. Then his brother snorted, too. They sounded like pigs and, come to think of it, they both had little pig noses, too.

I rolled my eyes. "Yeah," I said, "I've heard that joke before. My dad's the water coach on board. I know my name sounds funny when you first hear it—especially because I love the water . . . I even love baths." I forced myself to smile. I am trained to be polite to the paying guests.

Just as the boys reached for the drinks I was offering them, their aunt made a sweeping gesture with her arm. She bumped into me and knocked the glass of ginger ale out of my hand. It spilled all over her.

"Did you see that?" shouted Marie DeVaugn, pointing a finger at me. "That child just flung her drink at me!"

Her nephews just snickered. They had been watching and they knew that I hadn't done anything. The drinks had even been meant for them!

Camilla grabbed my arm. "Philippa, how dare you!!!"

That's when Philip stepped in. "It was an accident," said Philip. "I was watching. If it was anyone's fault, madam, it was yours. . . ."

"You . . . you . . . how dare you speak to me like that! I am a duchess. I am a descendent of none other than Marie Antoinette, the queen of France."

"I am the . . . ," said Philip. He was about to explain that he was the captain's son, when suddenly a high-pitched squeak came from the lady's handbag.

Philip and I looked at each other. I knew we had both heard it. Then something popped up out of the duchess's handbag. It looked like a bad toupee. The duchess tried to stuff it back into her handbag. But the yips kept coming.

Camilla Trout looked mortified. "Uh, excuse me, your grace," she said. "Is that a dog in your handbag?"

"That is Lady Windermere," said the duchess. "She is more of a person than a dog. She is a Havapoo."

"Have a poo?" asked Ruby.

"Have a poo?" repeated Sapphire.

Philip and I caught each other's eye and we burst out laughing.

The duchess gave us a dirty look. "A Havapoo is mixture of Havanese and poodle. The Havanese is the national dog of Cuba, and the Spanish aristocracy often had them in their homes. The poodle, as many of you know, also has rich royal history."

"The royal lineage of your dog is very interesting, as is yours," said Camilla, taking a deep breath. "But I am afraid that our rules on the ship are quite strict..." she paused. I knew Camilla was having trouble getting the words out. "The Havapoo will have to stay in the kennel."

"Lady Windermere! In a kennel!" said the duchess. "I don't think so! She is a pillow dog. She stays with me. After all, I am in the Royal Suite...."

"I know you're in the Royal Suite," said my mom. "But because of various quarantine rules in our ports of call, we have to keep all dogs in the kennels. Our cruise kennel, however, has quite the reputation for pampering our treasured four-footed guests."

I nodded. "The crew exercises the dogs in the early morning. Sometimes I help them. I love to do that."

"I will help, too," said Philip. "I have to walk my dog in the morning. My dog is traveling in the kennel as well. Perhaps Philippa and I could do it together."

The duchess sighed. She looked down. "Well," she said, "I suppose, Lady Windermere, if you are going to be taken care of by the captain's son . . . She is accustomed to being treated royally," warned the duchess.

"We'll do our best to make her happy," I said.

The duchess pushed the little ball of fluff into my arms. I felt as if the duchess wanted me to curtsy. The dog had on a ridiculous rhinestone collar that was almost bigger than she was. I patted the dog's head. She couldn't help the bad manners and bad taste of her owner. The duchess and her nephews swept through the Royal Promenade, not giving a backward glance at the little dog that was in my arms.

Philip and I walked out together onto the deck. I took Lady Windermere to the upper deck where the kennel was. It was that beautiful time of night when the sky had just turned dark.

At sea, the stars always seem to shine brighter. "There's Venus," I said to Philip. "Make a wish on the first star."

"It's not a star. It's a planet."

"Of course, I know that," I said. "But I still think it's beautiful. It's always pure white."

"Did you know that Galileo was the person who discovered that Venus has a cycle just like our moon?" Philip said.

"Did you know that Galileo was one of the first to see the four moons around Jupiter?" I asked, one-upping him. "That's how Galileo discovered that everything in the universe didn't circle the earth. That got him in a lot of trouble."

Philip gave me a little bow. "I should have guessed that a girl who lives at sea would know as much about the stars and planets as I do," he said.

"Yeah," I said, grinning. "Don't underestimate me, buddy."

Philip smiled. "Well, it's clear that we're both smart and perhaps we both like to show off a little," he admitted.

Just then there was a tremendous boom overhead. Philip ducked behind a lifeboat.

"Hey," I said, going over to him, "it's just the fireworks. We set them off whenever we start a voyage. You don't have to be afraid."

Philip dusted himself off. "I wasn't afraid," he said coolly.

I looked at him. His eyes told a different story; there was real fear in them.

"You know," I said, "you said you love mysteries. I have a mystery for you. The duchess said that she'd give up her dog because her pet would be taken care of by the captain's son. But you never told her you were the captain's son. So, how did she know that?"

Philip smiled at me. "You are actually good at this," he said.

I wasn't sure if he was teasing or not—or if he was genuinely surprised that I was good at solving mysteries. It would be fun to show him that I wasn't bragging.

CHAPTER THREE

ENEMIES—THAT'S A STRONG WORD

Early the next morning, I went to the kennel. Lady Windermere, the Havapoo, had lived up to her name. I cleaned up her mess, vowing to get to her earlier the next morning. I snapped the leash onto her bejeweled collar and took her out on deck. I have to admit that for a dog that looked like a toupee, she was kind of cute and spunky.

When I went out on the upper deck, I saw Philip with Maximillian. "Good morning," I said. I looked out at the sea. The first morning at sea is the most magical. The sky was lavender-pink. The sea was calm, and the great stabilizers that could keep our ship steady in even the biggest storms were turned off, so it was almost silent on the upper deck.

"I love it when it's this quiet," I said to Philip.

Maximillian sniffed the little Havapoo. Lady Windermere snapped at him. Maximillian splayed his long poodle legs in the play position. "He just wants to play," Philip said to the little dog.

"You ... you ... Havapoo! Play nice," I said to Lady Windermere.

Philip laughed. Lady Windermere gave me a trusting look. Her little bottom began to shake. I could tell she was wagging her tail, although it was hard to find her tail under all that hair.

"She looks happy now," I said.

"See? They can be friends," said Philip. "Now, I only wish the duchess could be more like her. She has already complained to my father that she doesn't think the security on the ship is good enough."

"The *Excalibur* is known as one of the safest cruise ships ever. We have the best safety record of any cruise ship," I said.

"I know," said Philip. "That was one reason my father was willing to let me come on this voyage."

"Why?" I asked. "Why is security so important?"

Philip bit his lip. "I wish you weren't so curious," he said.

I stared at him. "Hey," I said, "you said you liked mysteries. How can you like mysteries and not be curious?"

"I said I liked mysteries in *books*," said Philip.

"Captain Raynor gave me all his Agatha Christie mysteries," I bragged. I'll lend you *Death on the Nile*. It's cool because it takes place on a cruise ship."

"I love that in books the enemies are in the pages," said Philip, "and the detectives always win. In real life, sometimes the enemies win."

"*Enemies* . . . . That's a strong word. . . ," I said.

Philip looked out at sea. "Yes," he said. "Was it wrong? English isn't my first language."

"Your English is perfect," I said. "It's just that I wondered why you said *enemies*. Do you think you have enemies?"

"You really do ask a lot of questions," said Philip. "You're a question box."

"That's what Captain Raynor says about me. So, tell me more about Borgunlund," I said. "How old were you when you left there?"

"I was six," said Philip. He put his hand deep in Maximillian's fur. "Max was just a little puppy. He belonged to my mother. . . ."

Philip's voice drifted off. He was looking out at the horizon. Maximillian looked at me with his deep brown eyes. "Is your mother joining us later in the voyage?" I asked him.

"My mother is dead," said Philip.

"I am so sorry," I said. I felt like a fool.

Philip turned away from me abruptly. "I have to take Max back to the kennel. My father is waiting for me."

"Okay," I said. "I'll walk back with you."

Philip didn't wait for me. Poor Lady Windermere couldn't keep up with Max's long legs. We lost sight of them both.

Just as I turned the corner on the deck, I heard a voice, "Excuse me, little girl. I want to talk to you. . . ." It was the duchess. She was dressed in a purple and red caftan that had so many designs on it that it made me dizzy. I was worried that she had heard Philip and me talking about her.

"Philippa," said the duchess, "I am talking to you."

I gulped. I wasn't sure how she knew my name. I stopped short.

I didn't get it. Normally, paying customers don't have any real interest in the kids who are the children of the staff. We are kind of almost invisible.

"Philippa," repeated the duchess.

Maybe she was worried about her dog. I picked up little Lady Windermere in my arms. She wiggled in to make herself comfortable.

"Lady Windermere is just fine," I said.

"How nice," said the Duchess. She moved closer to me. There was something about the way she said *nice* that gave me the creeps. I turned around to go.

"You know," said the duchess, "I find it very interesting that you are friends with the captain's son."

Again, I couldn't figure out how she had found out so fast that Philip was the captain's son. Her voice was husky. It wasn't really threatening, but there was something flat and emotionless in her tone.

I wondered what she would think if she knew that Philip didn't like her very much.

She peered at me. "I think I recognize you from another cruise I took."

"My parents and I have sailed with the *Excalibur* ever since its maiden voyage. I don't remember you, Ma'am."

"I prefer that you call me by my proper name."

"Yes, Mrs. DeVaugn."

"Little girl, the proper way to address a duchess is as 'Your Grace.'"

I'm somewhat used to passengers treating me like a servant, but the way she was homing in on me was getting under my skin. I took a deep breath. I don't like being called little girl, but I knew I didn't want to make an enemy of her. It was funny . . . I had never thought of having enemies until Philip had used the word.

She lifted her sunglasses. Her eyes were pale blue, blank and unblinking. She looked at me like a butterfly collector looking at a specimen that she was going to pin to her collection. "We'll see each other again," she said.

"Yes, Your Grace." I nodded, but I wasn't looking forward to our next meeting.

CHAPTER FOUR

DANCING LIKE A PRINCESS

I put the little Havapoo back in her kennel, and took the private crew elevator back to our quarters. I wasn't in the mood to run into any more passengers. I got to the little two-room suite that I share with my parents. Our rooms don't have a porthole. Like most of the crew, we live below the waterline. Only the captain and officers have rooms with balconies, windows, or portholes. I picked up the Agatha Christie book that I had promised to Philip. I sat down on my bunk cross-legged and started to read the opening chapters.

I saw the handle to our door turning. I jumped.

"Hi, sweetheart," said Mom. She took a closer look at me. "What's wrong?" she asked. Mom always has a way of reading my mind. She sat down on the bunk beside me. "You were up early this morning,"

Mom stayed quiet. She often does that when she wants to give me time.

"It's not what you think," I said.

Mom gave me a quizzical look. "What am I thinking?"

"That I got in trouble with the Trout twins again and that Camilla is mad at me . . . ."

Mom is always hoping that I'll learn not to let Ruby and Sapphire get to me.

"That's not what I'm thinking," said Mom. "I was wondering if perhaps it was something with the captain's son. I hope you are getting along. He seems a little lonely. I'm sure that's why his father arranged for him to have his pets with him."

"He's confusing," I said. "I didn't know that his mother was dead. I don't think he liked my asking questions about her. He's a bit of a mystery."

"Well, he may be sensitive about his mother. That's understandable. Be a little patient with him."

"I'll try," I said. "He does love mysteries. I'm going to lend him one of the Agatha Christie books from Captain Raynor. He says he likes mysteries the way I do, but sometimes he acts almost like the duchess—like he thinks that he's so far above me."

"Nobody's really above you," said Mom. "Philip is the captain's son—not the captain. And I think he wants you to be his friend."

"I'm not sure he's quite a friend, yet," I said. "Sometimes he's fun and open . . . and then he goes all quiet."

"Like I said, give him a chance," said Mom. " Don't worry about his being the captain's son. After all, he's not royalty. Just be yourself. You're a wonderful friend."

"Speaking of royalty, the woman who calls herself a duchess seems way too interested in me and Philip," I said.

"Well, darling, you know passengers. They always show interest in the captain. They want to go home and brag that the captain became their *dear* friend. I wouldn't worry about it. And speaking of the captain, he'd like you to join him at the first sitting with Philip. Apparently Camilla has put the duchess and her nephews with him tonight, and he thought you would make a good addition to the young people. That's quite an honor. I told him that you would love to."

"Mom, I'm not sure. . . . I don't think I want to sit anywhere near the duchess."

Mom gave me a peculiar look. "Sweetheart, it doesn't matter. When the captain asks one of the crew to join him at the table, we do it. It's the captain's choice."

"Captain's choice," I said. I had heard those words all my life. The captain was the king as far as the ship was concerned and his orders were to be obeyed.

"And I'd like you to join me for the dance party before dinner," added Mom. "I'm giving a dance demonstration with your father. You always love the first night."

I do. All the passengers get dressed up, and Mom's dance team puts on a demonstration. I grinned at Mom. "You're right," I said. "I guess I'm just getting worked up about nothing, thinking about the duchess and Philip. "We've got a show to put on."

Mom gave me a little fist bump. "That's my girl," she said.

Later in the day, I got ready for the party. I put on my blue satin dress and my little Cuban heels. I have been allowed to wear little heels on my dancing shoes since I turned double digits, as Mom called it when I turned ten. I took the back elevator with Mom up to the ballroom.

Our ballroom is famous for having a beautiful inlaid-wood floor that is an exact replica of the ballroom floor on the *Titanic*. We also have a long, double-curved staircase that is a replica of the elegant staircase that was on the famous ship. You wouldn't think that passengers would like anything that would remind them of the most famous disaster at sea, but everyone loves to have their picture taken on the top of the staircase. Go figure. I noticed the duchess was posing at the top of the stairs.

I tried to avoid her. I had really had enough of the DeVaugns even though our journey had just begun. I watched my parents do their demonstration. Everyone applauded. Then the band began to play a tango. Mom asked for volunteers to learn the dance. I saw the duchess push Arthur toward Mom. Mom took him to the center of the floor to teach him. He didn't move well. There are little tricks that help you see if the woman is leading. Mom's hand on his shoulder was gripped tightly as she tried to maneuver Arthur around the floor. He probably danced better than he had ever before. I could see his body relaxing as Mom subtly led him.

His brother was standing in the corner, looking sullen. Part of my job is to try to make the passengers about my age feel at home, so I went up to him.

"Your brother seems to be enjoying himself," I said. "Would you like to dance?" He grunted. I took that as a yes.

The band began to play a merengue, which is much easier than the tango. I took his hand. Evan was absolutely the worst dancer I have ever danced with. In the merengue, you start on the two count—you're supposed to move your hips, not your shoulders. Evan's shoulders heaved as if they were on a seesaw. He couldn't take a step without stepping on my feet! Still, I tried to smile at him. He was wearing a blue blazer with gray pants. I noticed there were some loose threads on the pocket of his blazer. It looked like one of the blazers that some of the boys who go to prep schools wear, only theirs have a crest.

"Did you lose the crest on your jacket?" I asked. "Do you go to prep school? We get a lot of prep school kids."

Evan looked down at his jacket. "NO! I don't go to prep school, not that it's your business. You ask too many questions. Just dance." He stared down at his feet.

"Dancing is supposed to be fun," I said to him. "It's proper for partners to talk to each other, and you'll dance better if you lift your head up and look at me." I tried to smile.

Just then, the band changed rhythms. Philip came over to us and tapped Evan on the shoulder.

"What do you want?" asked Evan.

"I am cutting in," said Philip formally.

"What does that mean?" Evan asked.

Philip smiled at him. "It means that I, a gentleman, am asking to dance with your lady."

"She's not a lady," said Evan rudely. "She's just a girl who's here just because her parents work on the ship."

"And you are a boy without manners." Philip smiled.

Evan looked as if he wanted to wipe that smile off Philip's face. Were two boys getting into a fight over me? This was certainly something that had never happened before. Then Evan saw his brother, Arthur, motioning to him. "She's not a very good dancer anyway," he muttered, as he handed me off to Philip.

Philip gave me a little bow with his head, and we began to dance. Most boys my age don't know how to lead. Philip, however, held the perfect frame with a firm hand on my back. He dipped and danced to the music, making us look as if we were floating across the floor.

"Evan was wrong," said Philip. "You dance beautifully."

"Thank you," I said. "So do you."

"You look and dance like a princess," said Philip. I looked up at him. I could tell by his eyes that he was teasing, but it was a nice teasing.

Then I saw the duchess staring at us.

"The duchess is staring at you again," I said to Philip.

"I am the captain's son," said Philip, rather arrogantly. "People always stare at me."

He seemed so sure of himself. "You do dance beautifully," I told him. "Most boys our age can't do the waltz."

"My mother loved ballroom dancing," said Philip.

"I'm so sorry she didn't live to see what a wonderful dancer you are," I said. "But she taught you well."

Philip smiled at me. "Thank you." As the music ended, Philip gave me a little bow. People around us applauded as if we had done something very special. Adults always think that kids look so cute ballroom dancing, so it didn't surprise me that they were making a big deal out of us. It was still nice to get the applause— nice, that is, until I saw Marie DeVaugn glaring at us.

"That Marie DeVaugn is still staring at us," I said to Philip.

"We're having dinner with her tonight. Maybe we can do some detecting. Somehow she doesn't act like a real duchess should. Perhaps we can prove that she is not of royal blood."

"Not of royal blood," I said. "I like the sound of that...."

Philip looked at me. "Why?" he asked.

"Because she really gets under my skin," I said. "Some-times passengers treat us like second-class citizens."

"Us?" asked Philip.

"Well, maybe not you," I admitted. "The duchess keeps zeroing in on me," I said. "She's way too interested in me . . . and I like the idea that she isn't a duchess."

Philip held his hand out. "We will solve the mystery of the fake duchess together."

"It does sound like an Agatha Christie mystery," I said. "Oh, I have that book for you."

I took the little paperback out of my purse and handed it to him. When our hands touched, I felt as if an electric spark connected us. The fake duchess wasn't the only mystery on board. My feelings about Philip were a mystery, too.

CHAPTER FIVE

A CHOCOLATE MESS

Dinner at the captain's table is a lot more work than you'd think it would be. The service is very formal. All the waitstaff have to wear white gloves. Whenever I'm invited to sit at the captain's table, I have to be on my best behavior. And of course, just my luck, I was seated between Camilla and Arthur. The duchess was placed next to the captain. The only good thing was that Ruby and Sapphire had obviously been considered too young to sit at the captain's table with us.

"Ah, Captain," said the duchess, "this is indeed an honor. I am so sure we have met before. Were you the commodore on other cruise ships?"

Captain Vittiganen pulled out the chair for the duchess. "I regret that you are mistaken. I was an admiral in my country's small military, and I was also the captain for some of the largest container ships in the world. This is my first job on a passenger cruise line."

"Ah, an admiral," trilled the duchess. "I admire an admiral. However perhaps because you are used to the military, you haven't learned all the ins and outs of handling a cruise ship. I must say that I am very disappointed in your staff. I put my jewels in the safe in my room, and I noticed the maid making up my bed this morning was looking at me as if she wanted the combination."

"Yeah," said Arthur. "And Evan and I found the same maid poking around our room this afternoon . . . *after* it was cleaned this morning."

"Wait a minute," I said. "The maids are told to clean the rooms twice during the day. She was just doing her job. And we have turndown service during dinner."

"Well, it looked suspicious to me," said Arthur. "She was in there a long time."

The DeVaughns were making me angry. I was sure

that Evan and Arthur were the type who left their rooms a mess, lost things, and then blamed the staff. It happens all the time on the ship.

The duchess stared at Evan. "Darling, what happened to your family crest?" Evan didn't answer. He was too busy stuffing food into his mouth.

"You have a family crest?" asked Philip politely.

"Of course," said the duchess. "Every royal family has a family crest."

"I bet the maid that was snooping around our room snipped the crest off Evan's jacket," said Arthur.

"That's ridiculous," I blurted out. "Why would she do that?"

"The royal crest of the DeVaugn family is very famous in some circles," said the duchess. "It has a golden bird on it to represent the purity of our lineage."

"Many crests have birds on them," said the captain.

"Yes, but each is unique," said the duchess. "And I am so proud of our heritage. Captain Vittiganen, I'm sure you understand such pride. You are proud of your family's heritage, too, aren't you?"

The captain coughed into his elbow. "I am much

more interested in today than in the past," said the captain.

I smiled into my soup. It made me like the captain.

"Still," insisted the duchess, "the past is important. And I am very worried about my nephew's crest that has gone missing. I wouldn't be surprised if that maid did snip it. She will probably try to sell it on the Internet. Won't you do something?"

The captain frowned. "Madame, I am captain of the ship. If you have a housekeeping problem, you should bring it up with your steward," said the captain.

"I did, and the steward told me that the maid is his daughter. That did not leave me feeling very reassured."

I couldn't keep quiet. "Captain Vittiganen, the Arroyo family is in charge of the Royal Suite. They are very trustworthy. They've been with the ship forever. They started in the laundry. I know you're new on board, and you haven't gotten to know all of the people who work for you—but I can tell you that you couldn't have a family that is more loyal. You should trust them."

Camilla gave me a dirty look. There are many rules on a ship—and I was breaking most of them. You are never supposed to contradict a paying passenger—and you certainly are never supposed to tell the captain what he should do and whom he should trust.

Captain Vittiganen got very red in the face. For a moment I was afraid that he was going to tell me to leave the table immediately. But instead he turned on the duchess quite angrily.

"Madame, I think that young Philippa makes an excellent point. We have a wonderful staff on this ship. I regret that you had some discomfort and that your nephew is missing a crest on his pocket but, as the captain, I can assure you that you should feel as secure in your cabin as if you were in your own home."

Camilla interrupted, clearly worried about the direction of the conversation. "Duchess, may I offer you some champagne?" she said, reaching across me for the champagne that was in a wine bucket.

The duchess sighed. "Well, just a little," she said.

"Allow me," said the captain, taking the bottle from Camilla. As the captain lifted the champagne bottle,

Philip said, "Papa, may I be excused? Philippa is very interested in Amazonian parrots. May I invite her back to our quarters to spend time with Don Quixote? She is very good with animals."

I stared at him. I hadn't said anything about wanting to know more about Amazonian parrots. But maybe Philip had something that he wanted to tell me alone.

"It would be rude to exclude the other children at our table," said the captain after pouring the champagne. "Why don't all of you go visit the chocolate fountain instead?"

Philip made a face.

"The chocolate fountain!" shouted Evan. "That's something I want to see."

"Children, you are free to go," said the captain.

A captain may say something like "You are free . . ." and it sounds like you have a choice. But you don't. The captain was subtly ordering us to leave the table, and we were all to go together.

As we took the stairs to the upstairs lounge for dessert Philip took me aside. "I am proud of you for the way you stood up for the Arroyo family," he whispered.

"What you are two whispering about?" demanded Arthur.

"Yes, what are you talking about?" repeated Evan.

"Nothing," said Philip curtly. "Oh look, there's the chocolate fountain."

The chocolate fountain is on the aft deck that we call Floating Island. The centerpiece of the dessert table is a constantly flowing fountain in the shape of a three-headed swan. Instead of water flowing out of the swan's heads, out of one beak flows hot fudge, out of another a hot white-chocolate sauce, and out of another hot caramel.

Around the fountain are all the makings for the most fantastical sundae that you can think of—from banana splits, to sprinkles that glitter and glisten, to homemade peanut brittle. Evan looked like he was going to do a swan dive into the chocolate. He grabbed one of the gigantic sundae bowls and filled it with ice cream.

Ruby and Sapphire came up to us. They both looked

a little annoyed that they hadn't gotten to sit at the captain's table. "Hi, Philip," said Ruby. "Are you going to watch Philippa *fill up* with ice cream?"

"*Fill up* with ice cream!" said Evan, snorting so hard that ice cream came out of his nose.

"Yuck!" said Ruby.

"Yuck!" said Sapphire.

Evan reached into his pocket for a handkerchief to wipe his face. I looked down at the fountain. Something was floating in the caramel sauce. It looked like a leaf. I picked it out quickly before someone else saw it and complained to the staff.

I put it in a napkin. Then I looked down at it. It was the crest with the bird on it. I had to show it to Philip. I went over to him. Philip pointed at his mouth and held his hand up to ask for a moment while he swallowed. "I've got something important to show you," I said.

Philip nodded and put down his spoon. "What is it?" he asked.

"I need to show it to you privately," I said.

"Good," he said. "There is something I want to talk

to you about anyhow. Let's go to my quarters. Nobody will disturb us there."

"We'll have to be sneaky," I whispered to Philip. "Otherwise, the rest of them will follow us."

"Don't worry," said Philip. "I can be sneaky when I want to." He gave me a wink.

CHAPTER SIX

DO MY BIRDS SCARE YOU?

"**H**ey," shouted Ruby, "where are you two going?"

"Yeah, where are you going?" repeated Sapphire.

I sighed. "So much for being sneaky," I whispered to Philip. "We'll never get rid of the twins. They stick like Velcro."

"Don't worry," Philip whispered back. "I will get rid of them." He turned to the twins and said, "I'm afraid that I must call it a night. Philippa, I have that book that you were asking about in my cabin."

I hadn't asked about any book. In fact, it was the other way around. I was going to lend Philip another one of Captain Raynor's Agatha Christie books.

"Oh, right," I lied.

"Hey," said Arthur, "I've always wanted to see where the captain sleeps."

I spoke up. "The fanciest stateroom is the duplex that you're in. It's the one where celebrities stay. You've got your own elevator and terrace. Isn't that enough for you?"

Arthur swallowed his ice cream. "Well, yes, of course. I know our suite is nice, but I want to see the captain's quarters, too."

I looked at him suspiciously. Everyone in the De-Vaugn family seemed unusually interested in the captain and his son.

"Follow me," said Philip. "I would be glad to show you."

I tagged behind Philip. "Why did you invite them?" I whispered to him.

"I told you I have something that I have to show you privately. Trust me," he whispered back. "They won't stay long, and then we will be alone."

"You two are always whispering together," said Sapphire.

"Yes," said Arthur with a snort. "Ha! Ha! They are

like horse whisperers ... because their names mean lover of horses. That's what Philip and Philippa means in Greek." He snorted again.

The snort wasn't pretty, but I was impressed that he knew that our names meant 'lover of horses.' Arthur acted like someone who wasn't very smart, but I had a feeling that he was a lot smarter than he let on. He had a way of watching me that reminded me of his aunt, the duchess.

Philip led us directly to the elevator that is reserved for officers and the staff instead of the more posh mahogany-paneled elevators for the passengers.

When we stepped out of the elevator, we walked a little ways down the hallway until we got to the captain's room. Philip put his room key card into the slot and opened the door to his quarters. My mouth dropped open. We all stood with our mouths open.

"Is anything wrong?" Philip asked.

"It just looks so different," I said.

I'd been to the captain's quarters many times when Captain Raynor was the captain. Back then, the captain's quarters were shipshape and almost bare-boned, except for Captain Raynor's book collection. Now the captain's quarters looked like a palace. There were oriental rugs on top of rugs, and there were so many birds in cages it was hard to move.

There was a loud squawking noise. I whirled around. When I looked closer at the birds I realized that none of them were real. But they were all making loud noises. They were made out of metal but were incredibly ornate, like works of art, and their eyes looked like jewels.

"Can you find the real bird?" asked Philip. He seemed to be throwing it out as a challenge to all of us. He laughed, but it wasn't a very nice laugh.

Through the incredible noise, I looked through the menagerie of mechanical birds. All were painted bright colors. In a corner by the computer, I heard one voice squawking, "Kiem *say*." Slowly I moved over toward the computer.

"Don Quixote." I looked into the cage. A pair of very lively black eyes looked back at me. I had found the real parrot.

Don Quixote nodded. He cocked his majestic head

as if hoping that I understood what was going on around me. But I didn't.

Just then Arthur flapped his arms at one of the mechanical birds. Then he jumped back. The bird's wings were motorized, and they flapped back at him, making whirligig motions. One seemed to set off the others . . . and soon every bird's metal wings flapped in the air.

"Stand still!" ordered Philip.

Suddenly the awful noise stopped. Philip smiled at me, but I wasn't exactly sure what was so funny or where he was going with this. What was the purpose of the birds? And why had he invited us all back to see them?

"This is creepy," said Evan.

Even Arthur looked creeped out.

Philip smiled at Arthur. "Did you enjoy your visit to the captain's quarters? Perhaps you wish that I were a bird whisperer, not a horse whisperer."

Arthur glared at him.

"Now, if you don't mind," said Philip, "I want to talk to Philippa alone."

He sounded as if he were ordering them, not asking.

"You are a very weird dude," said Arthur as he was leaving.

"Weird dude," repeated Sapphire. Ruby nodded. They both looked a little scared. I didn't blame them.

"I take that as a compliment," said Philip.

Philip looked at me as they filed out the door. "I told you that I would get rid of them."

"Yes," I said, "but I don't understand. What is the purpose of these birds?"

"Do my birds scare you?"

"I don't scare easily," I said.

"No, you don't. . . ." said Philip.

I sighed. The more I saw of Philip, the more confusing he was. "These creatures are amazing," I said. "I've never seen anything like them."

"They are very old burglar alarms," said Philip. "If someone makes a sudden move around them and the alarm system is on, they start to flap their wings and squawk." Philip smiled. "They belonged to my mother. I inherited them."

"Well, they are unique," I admitted.

"My mother loved parrots," said Philip. "She inherited these mechanical birds from her mother. They have been in our family for generations. They originally were a gift from the Emperor of China, and then they were handed down to my mother's family."

"And these birds were designed to scare people?" I asked.

"They were for amusement," said Philip. "But they are also . . . how do you say . . . scarecrows."

I laughed. "There is nothing wrong with your English."

"Thank you," said Philip. "I must admit, I enjoyed scaring those annoying boys and those two little Trouts."

I should have been happy that he didn't like the Trout twins, but somehow he sounded too pleased with himself—almost as if by being the captain's son, he had the right to dislike anybody who worked for his father.

"Well, they *are* younger than we are," I said, suddenly feeling defensive of the twins.

"Yes, but you have to admit they are annoying."

I wanted to tell him that he could be annoying, too.

He had all the privileges of the captain's son, and some-times he seemed to relish it a bit too much. He got to live in this magnificent cabin with the best views of the ocean that money could buy.

"You know what, I've got to go, too," I said. I really didn't want to stick around when Philip was ordering everyone around.

"No, wait," said Philip.

I glared at him. "I don't take orders," I said.

"Please," said Philip. "You can't go. You must show me what you were going to show me. Remember, you said you have something important to show me."

"Yes," I said. "But if we're really going to be friends and detectives together, you can't go ordering me around the way your father can order our crew. Your father is captain, not you . . . ."

To my surprise Philip laughed. "I wish my mother had met you. She would like the way you talk to me."

"She would?" I asked.

"You don't let me pull rank," he said.

I looked at his desk. Sitting at a prominent position on his desk was a picture of a beautiful woman with blond hair. She was holding a young baby on her lap, and the smile on her face was glowing.

"Is that your mother?" I asked softly. "She was beautiful."

Philip nodded. "Please, Philippa, won't you show me what you were going to show me? I'm asking, not commanding."

I sighed. Somehow the missing crest on Evan's pocket seemed like a simple mystery compared with the mysterious Philip. I pulled out the napkin that held the caramel-covered crest. "This fell out of Evan's pocket."

"Let me see it," said Philip. He took some hand sanitizer and gently dabbed at the crest with a tissue. It didn't seem to hurt the colors of the crest. He rubbed a little harder. I peered over his shoulder.

"I'm sure this was the crest that was on Evan's jacket. He lied about not knowing where it was . . ." I paused. Philip was staring at the golden bird. He seemed very still. "Do you recognize it?" I asked Philip.

"Why would I recognize it?" he demanded, once again taking that tone that I didn't like.

Then he burped. "Excuse me. I'm so sorry."

"It's okay."

He burped again. He was looking a little green.

"Are you okay?" I asked him.

"I don't know," he said. "I feel a little queasy. Maybe I ate too much ice cream."

"Well, if anyone was going to get a stomachache, you'd think it would be Evan or Arthur. They were like pigs at the ice cream fountain," I said.

Philip didn't answer me. There was something about the way his shoulders slumped that made me think he really didn't feel well.

"Are you okay?"

"Yeah, I think so, but I need to lie down. Do you mind leaving?"

"Of course not," I said.

Philip looked up at me. "Would you do me a favor?" he asked. "Take Maximillian for a walk tomorrow morning? I think I'm getting seasick."

"But the sea is calm," I said. "Do you get seasick often?"

"Never," said Philip. "Please . . . I really don't feel well."

"Okay, but if you feel better in the morning, come join me. Maybe the air will do you good."

Philip raised his head. He smiled again. He picked up the book I had lent him. "Maybe if I read this book, I will feel better," he said. He started to read. But he still looked green. And I was sure that Philip had recognized something in the golden bird on the crest that had disturbed him. I just didn't know why.

CHAPTER SEVEN
YOU'D THINK THEY WERE REAL DIAMONDS

I love being out and about on the ship in the hours before dawn. The public areas of the ship are almost empty. Oh, there are always a few passengers who have gambled late or are taking a stroll because they are having a shipboard romance. Still, in the hours before dawn you can feel as if you have the great ship all to yourself. The stars were fading, and the sky was turning that slight tinge of lavender that it gets before dawn. I entered the kennel.

Maximillian and Lady Windermere both greeted me. Lady Windermere's little body was twitching with anticipation. I have to admit that I was happy to see her—maybe she was as tiny as a fungus, but she was growing on me. I put on her ridiculous rhinestone collar. Then I went to Maximillian's cage. His collar was already attached so I clipped on the two leashes and took the dogs out as the sun was just starting to rise. The sea was calm, and our great ship was making good time. I took both dogs for a walk on the deck.

As usual, there were a few folks jogging around the upper deck. They smiled at me with the two dogs. We went by the breakfast buffet with its cornucopia of fruits cascading out of a great basket, croissants and pastries. It all looked delicious but I couldn't have any. Unless I am specifically asked to accompany a guest to a meal, I eat my breakfast in the crew mess below deck.

I took the dogs past the caged-in tennis courts and golf driving range. The dogs wagged their tails in the breeze. I walked around to the portside of the ship, near the bridge and the captain's quarters. I thought about knocking on Philip's door to see how he was. But if he was really sick, he probably needed his sleep. Was he really sick, or had he just gotten into one of his moods? Maybe he didn't really like me standing up to him. Or was he just trying to hide what he knew about the crest from me? There was so much that I couldn't figure out. I sat down on an out-of-the-way deck chair.

Suddenly I got a whiff of a really pungent perfume and I was confronted by the duchess, with Evan and Arthur following her.

"Good morning, my little darling," said the duchess. I knew she wasn't talking to me. She knelt down beside Lady Windermere.

"Oh, my little sweetums, did this little girl put on the wrong collar? No wonder you look so uncomfortable."

Before I could stop her, the duchess had taken off Maximillian's collar and put it on Lady Windermere. To my surprise it fit. I guess all of Lady's Windermere's hair made her collar as big as Max's.

Arthur grabbed the leash for Lady Windermere from my hand. "I'll take her back to the kennel."

"Hey, wait a minute," I said. I grabbed onto the leash. Arthur tugged. One of the rhinestones on the collar came loose.

"Let go," Arthur hissed at me. "I am not kidding."

Just then Camilla came by. She saw me having a tug-of-war over the leash with the duchess and her nephews.

"Philippa, what is going on here?" she demanded.

I was completely flummoxed.

"Well," I said in a shy voice, "this collar was on Maximillian this morning. I was walking the duchess's dog and the captain's dog. The duchess thinks the collars were mixed up. But . . ."

Camilla looked angry. "Philippa, I will not have you arguing with one of our guests."

I just knew that I couldn't let the duchess have Maximillian's collar. "Camilla, that's the wrong collar," I said. "That collar belongs to Maximillian. Maximillian means so much to both the captain and Philip."

"This little girl is nothing but trouble," said the duchess. "Why should she care about a silly rhinestone collar?"

I wasn't going to give up. "Camilla, at least let me go get Philip before you let her have the collar," I said.

"Philippa," hissed Camilla, "don't make trouble."

I didn't care. The duchess was not getting Maximillian's collar. I *was* going to make trouble. I ran to the door of the captain's quarters.

"What are you doing?" demanded Camilla.

The captain opened the door. Maximillian bounded like a deer over to the captain.

"What is going on?" Captain Vittiganen asked. "Philip isn't feeling well. He said he got a stomachache last night."

"Please, Captain," I begged. "It's about Maximillian's collar. I know he came on board with this collar . . . and it belongs to you."

"Father?" I heard a voice. Philip came to the door. He was wearing silk pajamas that had peacock feathers printed on them.

"What's the matter?" Philip asked me. I tried not to stare at his pajamas.

"The duchess wants Max's collar," I said. "The duchess insists that I mixed them up. But I didn't want her to get yours—in case the collar has sentimental value."

Philip looked at the collar that was now on Maximillian.

"Father, maybe Philippa is right. It's odd that the two collars look so much alike. But Mom had that collar especially made for Max."

"I think I would know the collar on my own little dog that I've had since it was a puppy," said Duchess DeVaugn in her haughtiest voice.

The captain sighed. "Madame, I don't think this is worth the fuss that you are making of it. Camilla, please make sure that I am not bothered by such petty problems anymore." He looked at Philip and then at me. "Let us not make an issue of this." There was something about his voice that made it sound much more like an order.

"Philippa, please apologize to the duchess," insisted Camilla.

"This little girl makes such a fuss .... You would think they were real jewels," the duchess complained.

The captain smiled at the duchess. "Madame," he said, "we all know that's not true. Who would put real jewels on a dog?"

"Why, no one," said the duchess. She laughed.

The captain nodded. I felt as if I were watching a

chess game and I wasn't exactly sure who was about to get checkmated.

"I wouldn't want you to think that my family is so foolish as to put jewels on a dog," said the captain. "If you insist that Maximillian's collar got switched, your dog can keep both collars."

The duchess looked angry. "Well, of course, it really doesn't make much of a difference. I just wanted to make sure. Arthur, you can let this girl take both dogs back. We should have our breakfast."

Arthur handed me the leash to Lady Windermere. I wanted to slap him across the face. I felt Philip come up behind me and put pressure on my arm. The duchess gave me one of her unblinking stares. I wished I knew what was going on. The duchess and Arthur left, leaving me alone with Philip.

"She did take Maximillian's collar," I insisted. "She wanted it. . . ."

"I know," said Philip. "I saw the way the duchess was looking at the collar. She really believed that they were diamonds."

"That's ridiculous. Who would put diamonds on a

dog?" I asked him. "The ship has a safe in each room, and even movie stars keep their valuables in the safes."

"You are right," said Philip. "It is ridiculous. Just promise me, Philippa, that you won't do anything to get the duchess angry. You could be in real trouble."

"What kind of trouble?" I asked him.

"Please," begged Philip, "no more questions until I feel better."

CHAPTER EIGHT

THE ROYAL CREST OF BORGUNLUND

I knew if I wanted answers I would have to find them myself. There was one adult that I could count on not to treat my questions as silly. I went in search of Captain Raynor.

I found him in the computer room.

"Philippa," he said, smiling, "are you here to a get a head start on our studies?"

"Well, yes, if you promise that we'll study Borgunlund," I said.

Captain Raynor smiled at me. "Are you interested in Borgunlund or in the Captain's son?" he teased me.

"Borgunlund!" I insisted. "You're the one who taught me that it was a good thing to be curious about the people we meet at sea."

"Touché!" said Captain Raynor. "You are right. And actually, I had to refresh my memory about Borgunlund when I learned that was the Captain and his son's homeland."

"So what should I know about Borgunlund?" I asked him.

"I know that they were ruled by royalty for centuries," said Captain Raynor. "Then there were many revolutions, not long after the Russian Revolution. Many of the royal family lost their heads. There was still turmoil in the late twentieth century—it's really not so very long ago."

"Is Borgunlund famous for its diamonds?"

"I really don't know" said Captain Raynor. "Why don't you ask Philip? He is the one who would know the most about Borgunlund."

I reached into my pocket and brought out the loose stone that had come off Maximillian's collar.

"That's quite a stone," said Captain Raynor. "Where did you get it?"

"It's a rhinestone that fell off Max the dog's collar. But if it *was* real, how could I find out?"

"Who would put a real diamond on a dog?" asked Captain Raynor.

"I know it sounds silly, but if it *were* real how would I know? I'm sure this is fake . . . but I need to prove it to somebody."

"Well," said Captain Raynor, "the only people who can authenticate a real diamond are jewelers. You could take it to the jewelry shop."

The ship had a jewelry shop that carried diamonds and jewelry worth millions of dollars. But I knew how much people on the ship gossiped. If I went to the jewelry shop, asking about the diamond that had fallen off Max's collar, it would be all over the ship.

"At the jewelry store, they'll want to know where I got this stone. Isn't there an easier way?" I asked Captain Raynor. "I thought I read that if you try to scratch a diamond along glass, it will scratch, but a fake diamond won't.

"No, don't do that!" shouted Captain Raynor, holding up his hand. "That's a myth. Although it's true that diamonds are the hardest organic substance on earth, the infamous test of scratching diamonds across glass or metal might just give you a damaged diamond."

I looked at the stone in my hand. "Well, if it's a real diamond, I wouldn't want to do that."

"Well, there *are* a few easy tests we can do without any special equipment. I guess we could call this a science experiment."

"Good," I said. "You know I like science."

"Breathe on the stone. If it turns foggy, it isn't real."

I took a deep breath. I blew on the stone.

Captain Raynor and I both stared at it. The stone didn't look as bright.

"It's a rhinestone," said Captain Raynor.

"Oh," I sighed.

"You sound disappointed," said Captain Raynor. "What's going on, Philippa? Where did you get this stone?"

"I told you, it fell off Maximillian's collar," I said. "The Duchess DeVaugn made a grab for it. For a moment, I thought it might be real."

"Come on, Philippa," said Captain Raynor. "You can't

really think that a dog collar would be made of real diamonds. Even some of the movie stars that we've had on board wouldn't do that."

"But the duchess is way too interested in Philip."

"Philippa, you've been on ship long enough to know that everyone is interested in getting to know the captain. When they go home they like to brag that the 'dear captain' became their great friend."

"That's what Mom said," I admitted. I stared at the stone.

"Is there another test to see if a stone is a real diamond? Maybe our first test failed."

"Try putting it over this newspaper," said Captain Raynor. "Diamonds refract so much light that, if it's real, you should not be able to see through it. Other clear stones like glass or crystal will reveal the print clearly."

I looked at the newspaper. I could see the words clearly.

"It's not real, is it?" I asked.

"No," said Captain Raynor. "Philippa, maybe you should forget about diamonds for now."

"I have another thing I want to look up," I said.

Captain Raynor smiled at me. "Well, there is nothing wrong with curiosity. What is it?"

"I've got a hunch," I said. I took out the crest that had fallen off Evan's pocket. "Is this the crest of Borgunlund?" I asked.

Captain Raynor picked up the crest. "It's sticky," he said.

"I know," I said. "It's got caramel sauce on it."

I went to the computer and typed "crest of Borgunlund" into the search engine. The crest had a picture of a golden bird on it.

"Look at this, Captain Raynor!" I said. "The crest of Borgunlund and this crest are the same! Philip must have recognized it. Why didn't he tell me?"

Captain Raynor looked up and turned to the door. "You can ask him yourself," he said. "There he is."

I looked up. Philip was standing at the door to the computer room. He still didn't look well.

"Are you all right?" I asked him.

"Better," he said. "What are you doing?"

"I found an important clue," I said. "The duchess's

crest looks exactly like the one from Borgunlund. I don't know how you didn't recognize it."

"Maybe I was too sick," said Philip.

Captain Raynor looked concerned. "Did you see a doctor?" he asked.

"I didn't need a doctor," said Philip.

Philip slowly sat down at the computer. "That's the crest of Borgunlund," I said to him. "And this is the crest that the duchess claims is from her royal family. They look very much alike. Do you think she's from Borgunlund?"

"NO!" snapped Philip. "Definitely not!"

Captain Raynor and I looked at each other.

"Then why is the crest the same?" I asked. "I don't think it's a coincidence."

"That's ridiculous," said Philip. "Now you are letting your love of mysteries go too far."

I narrowed my eyes at him. "You said you love mysteries, too."

"May I talk to you alone?" Philip whispered.

"We can trust Captain Raynor," I whispered back.

"Please," asked Philip, "I'm begging you. I want to

speak to you in private." He had never begged before. It didn't really come naturally to him.

I sighed. "Captain Raynor, thanks for your help. But I think Philip needs some fresh air."

Captain Raynor smiled at us. "Good idea. Go outside and enjoy the sea breezes. Tomorrow we reach San Aurelia. And after that our real classes will begin."

"Thank you, sir," said Philip. He really did still look a little green.

"Are you sure you don't get seasick?" I asked him.

"What's wrong with me is NOT from being seasick!" said Philip. Now he sounded like the old Philip again.

CHAPTER NINE
JEOPARDY MEANS DANGER

Philip held the door open for me. We went out onto the deck.

"Let's get something straight," I said when we were alone. "One, you are not in charge of me. And two, the crest on Evan's jacket is the crest of Borgunlund. There's no way you didn't recognize it. Why did you tell Captain Raynor that you didn't? And what about last night? Did you pretend to be sick just to get rid of me?"

"That's what I came to tell you," said Philip. "I needed to be alone. I was shocked when I saw that the crest came from my homeland. I am sure the DeVaugns are not from Borgunlund. It's a very small country, and I knew all the royalty from my country."

"How did you know all of the royalty?" I asked.

"Every schoolboy in Borgunlund knows the royal families," said Philip dismissively. "But forget about the crest for a minute. I think the DeVaugn family didn't want me to walk Maximillian this morning. I don't think it was an accident that I got sick last night. My father called the ship's doctor. Nobody else who ate the ice cream or any of the food got sick. I think that they put something in my food to make me sick."

"So that they could switch the collar? That doesn't make sense," I said. "Who would want a dog collar? Philip, I think you know more about this than you've told me."

"I have told you everything that I know," said Philip.

I didn't really believe him, but I realized I wasn't going to get anywhere if I pushed him. I decided to not ask any more questions for a while. We walked past a sign for a shipboard *Jeopardy!* tournament for 4:00 P.M.

Philip stared at the sign. It had my mother's name on it as the person who would be leading the game.

"Your mother is the mistress of jeopardy?" he asked me.

The way he said it was so funny. "Mistress of *Jeopardy!*?" I repeated.

"*Jeopardy* is not a joke, is it?" asked Philip.

"It's a game," I said to him. "It's been on television forever. Don't tell me you've never played *Jeopardy!*"

"I've played jeopardy," said Philip defensively, "but never as a game. . . ."

"What does that mean?" I asked him.

"Nothing," said Philip. "Doesn't 'jeopardy' mean danger?"

"It does," I said. "Why?" I teased. "Do you think we're in danger? I can protect us. I know karate. My father teaches it on board. I've been doing karate since I was five. I am a brown belt," I said.

"I thought he did water sports," said Philip.

I smiled at Philip. "Most people who work on a ship do more than one thing. My mom is the dance teacher, and she does *Trivial Pursuit* and the *Jeopardy!* game. Dad teaches water sports, but he also teaches karate class and when we get to San Aurelia, he's in charge of taking the guests horseback riding."

"So do you do all those things, too?" asked Philip.

I nodded a little proudly. "Well, I love to ride, and I've been doing karate since I was five."

Philip looked very thoughtful. "Could you teach me to do karate?" he asked.

"It takes years to master. I could teach you the beginnings of it, though. But first you were going to tell me your secret."

Philip nodded. "My father does not want me to get too close to you."

"That's a little insulting," I said. "I thought your father liked me. He's been very nice to me."

"It's not that," he said. "He does like you, but he said that I should be careful in order to protect you."

"From what? Philip . . . please tell me . . . ."

"I would feel better if I could protect myself."

"I will teach you only if you stop being so secretive," I told him.

Philip smiled at me. I had to admit that he had the nicest smile. "Please," he said, "I am finally feeling better. I need to get some exercise."

We went to the workout rooms. I looked at the

schedule. Nobody was expected in this room until five o'clock. I went to the closet and got out a clean *gi* for Philip.

The belt was stiff. Philip frowned. "I don't want to wear a white belt," he said. "Doesn't it come in another color?"

I laughed at him. "This isn't like royalty. You aren't born into a rank in the martial arts. You have to earn your ranking—white, yellow, green, purple, brown, black."

I went into the bathroom to put my own *gi* on.

When I came out, Philip looked at me critically. "Your belt—it's dirty," he said, staring at my frayed brown belt.

"It's not dirty," I said with a smile. "It's worn. You never wash your belt. It's a badge of honor. The sweat you put into it makes you proud of it. The only time you change it is when you earn a higher color. Go change," I said to Philip, "and I'll meet you in the practice room." Philip turned to go. I liked giving him orders for a change.

CHAPTER TEN

KARATE!

I walked into the practice room. The lights were off. I flicked them on, and that's when I felt a warm hand clamp over my mouth. I tried to scream. The hand was over my nose. My eyes opened. For a second I thrashed around like a fish.

Then I tried to calm down. Dad had taught me that panic was my enemy—in all situations. He had taught me to take care of myself.

I pretended to go slack. When my body went slack, I felt the person behind me bend their knees with my deadweight, which gave me the chance I was looking for. I stomped down with my right foot...hard onto the foot of my attacker. The instep is one of the most sensitive areas of a person's body—that and the kneecap. I kicked back again with my left foot.

"Hey!" I heard a growl behind me. The grip on my mouth came off.

I whirled around. It was Arthur! He was struggling to get his breath back. I looked around the room.

Evan had Philip down on the floor. I grabbed Evan by the back of his uniform and got him off Philip. I flipped Evan onto the mat, and he struggled to get up. I stood over him.

Philip was on the floor and was as white as the wall.

"Don't move," I warned Evan. "I want to know what's going on!"

Evan raised his head "My brother and I were just practicing karate," he said in a whiny voice. "You surprised us."

"What were you doing practicing in the dark?" I demanded. I looked over at Arthur, who was rubbing his instep where I had stepped on him.

"It was her father who told us to practice in the dark," said Evan, pointing at me.

"Don't be ridiculous," said Philip. "Philippa's father would never suggest something like that."

I took a deep breath. "Actually, it's not ridiculous. It's kind of true. Dad often teaches students to practice in the dark. That way you learn to trust your other senses and not rely just on sight."

I looked at Arthur and Evan. They were dressed in clean white karate uniforms, and Arthur was wearing a purple belt. Evan was wearing a green belt.

"They attacked you," whispered Philip. "And they attacked me."

"I know," I said. "But don't forget they're paying customers."

"Perhaps we did interrupt your training session," said Philip smoothly. "If so, we apologize. I am a beginner. But I understand that Philippa here is an expert, as is her father. Perhaps you should take lessons from her as well as her father, since she seems to have taken both of you and won!"

"It wasn't fair. She had me at an unfair advantage . . . ," said Arthur.

"Unfair advantage!" I laughed. "You grabbed me from behind—made a surprise attack—nothing like a real karate match. You clapped your arm around my nose, another illegal karate move."

"You kicked me," said Arthur. "That wasn't fair."

Philip started to laugh. "Excuse me," he said. "Perhaps I am the one who knows the least about karate. But isn't the karate kick part of the art form?"

"It's balance . . . and skill," I said proudly.

Arthur gave me a dirty look. "It was luck," he snarled.

"Do you want a rematch?" I asked.

He glared at me. He grabbed his brother's arm, and they left the room. Philip and I were left alone. Philip rubbed his elbow. "Are you all right?" I asked him. "For someone with no training, you tackled Evan pretty quickly."

"I was angry," said Philip. "I didn't like to see you attacked—but you proved you can take care of yourself.

He bowed to me. I bowed back.

"We are a good team," said Philip.

"A good team trusts each other," I said to Philip.

"Don't you trust me?" asked Philip.

"I trust you," I said. "I just think you know more about the DeVaugn family and Borgunlund than you are telling me."

Philip looked at his feet. He didn't answer me.

CHAPTER ELEVEN

ON YOUR HIGH HORSE

I couldn't sleep much that night. I got up just before dawn. I was up early, but not as early as Captain Raynor. I found him on the upper deck. He was looking out at sea. He smiled at me. "Look at the seagulls," he said. "We're getting close."

"You were the one who taught me that Columbus knew he was getting close to land when he saw the birds," I said to him.

Captain Raynor grinned. "True, but if you've been at sea as many times as I have, you can just smell land. Even the air smells different. You don't realize it before you sail, but land smells sweet. On the ocean there is nothing but the smell of salt mixed in with the air."

"Do you miss being in command?" I asked him.

He stretched. "No," he said. "I miss the sea much more than I miss being in control. I thought it might be awkward for the new captain to have me on board. And in my head, I was thinking this might be my last voyage, but he's a good man."

"A little mysterious, though," I said. "Or at least his son is. . . ."

"You are together all the time. I thought you were such good friends."

"Kind of," I said. "But I don't think he really trusts me. I know there's something very strange about Duchess DeVaugn. There's some connection to Borgunlund that I just know that Philip knows, but he won't tell me."

"Don't push him," said Captain Raynor. "This can't be easy for him, leaving his homeland, losing his mother . . . give him time . . . ."

"Are you telling me to be patient?" I asked.

Captain Raynor grinned at me. "Well, Philippa, you

have lots of wonderful qualities—curiosity, energy, you're a good soul—but patience is not your long suit."

"What does that mean, long suit?" I asked. "I don't get it...."

"Someday I'll have to teach you bridge," said the captain.

I laughed. "Doesn't that take patience?" I asked. The bridge players among the passengers often played for hours.

"Yes," said Captain Raynor. "That's why it'll be a good game for you."

"Okay," I said. "But first, I have to take Lady Windermere for her walk."

Captain Raynor laughed. "I didn't mean this minute. I'll see you after we anchor at the island."

I got Lady Windermere out of the kennel. She sniffed the air. I wondered if she could smell land, too. "We'll take a long walk today," I said to her, "because I'll be gone all day."

She wagged her tail.

Philip joined me at the kennel. "I saw you talking to

Captain Raynor," he said. "What were you talking about?"

"Patience," I said. Philip took Maximillian out of the crate.

"Patience is a good thing," he said. "My father is always trying to teach me patience."

"Maybe it's just something that comes naturally to people who become captains," I said. "Captain Raynor is a very patient man. So maybe, if I learn it, I could become captain."

"And I will be your first mate," said Philip, giving me a mock salute. I couldn't tell if he was making fun of the idea or not.

I laughed. "You seem to be in a good mood today."

"I'm feeling so much better this morning," said Philip. "And I am excited. My father gave me permission to go on shore because the cruise ship owns the island. We can swim and just hang out and stop worrying about the duchess and Arthur and Evan."

"I can't just hang out," I said. Philip just assumed that I was just like him, the captain's son with all the privileges he enjoyed. "I'm helping my father take a group of people horseback riding." I wanted Philip to know that not everybody could just take a day off, even kids.

"I will go with you! I love to ride horses. My mother was a champion. She actually rode in the Olympics for Borgunlund."

"Wow!" I said. I suddenly felt badly that I had been feeling jealous of Philip. After all, I had both my mom and dad and, even though we didn't get along every minute, I knew they loved me. "Your mother sounds wonderful—a ballroom dancer, an Olympic champion."

"Yes, she was wonderful," said Philip simply.

I could tell that talking about his mother made him sad. I tried to change the subject. "You will love riding at San Aurelia. We get to ride on the beach because my father plans the ride for low tide so the sand is hard and packed."

"What are the horses like on the island?" Philip asked, seeming glad to talking about something other than his mother.

"Well, some of them get fat on the salt grass. My very favorite is Sir Galahad. He's very spirited. Not too many of the passengers can ride him, so I usually get him."

"Will there be a good horse for me?" Philip asked.

"Well, they always get some new ones. Dad will decide."

Philip frowned. I could tell he was used to always getting the best horse.

"What kind of horse did your mother ride?" I asked him.

"She rode a beautiful Arabian stallion," said Philip. "He was a retired racehorse." Philip stopped talking. As so often happened when he talked about his mother or his family, his voice just trailed off. We walked silently around the deck with the dogs. It was funny how in just a few days, the little Havapoo and the poodle were now getting along so well. They walked together, both their heads up in the air.

After we got the dogs back in the kennel, I told Philip I would meet him in the lounge where the passengers who have signed up for shore excursions go. Then I began helping my father check the list of the people who wanted to go riding. There was a gentleman who was dressed in proper riding jodhpurs and knee-high riding boots. It sometimes shocks me how much luggage people bring with them.

Just as we were checking names off our list, Philip came down to join us. He too wore jodhpurs and a per-fectly cut, red riding jacket. He was carrying a beauti-ful English saddle and a crop.

"Good morning, Philip," said Dad. "You don't really need your own saddle."

"I always ride on my own saddle," said Philip. "It be-longed to my mother."

"It could get wet," said my father. "We ride along the beach."

"I will bring it. I will take care of it."

Dad sighed. He had too many details to take care of to try to talk Philip out of bringing the saddle.

"As you wish," he said. "My guess from your outfit is that you have ridden before."

"I'm an expert," said Philip. Dad nodded and turned to the other passengers.

"Your father looked as if he didn't believe me," whis-pered Philip.

"Lots of people tell us they are experts," I said. "In fact, most of the time, adults lie about their experience much more than kids do. And Dad has a lot to take care of. This is a working day for him, not a vacation," I said.

"I do not lie," said Philip, still sounding petulant.

"Drop it," I said to him. "We all have work to do."

Philip looked at me. His mood changed. "You are right," he said. "I like the way that you don't treat me as special. I was acting a little spoiled. I am sure that you are a good rider, too. After all, you and I are both named for the Greek god who loved horses."

He held his pinkie out to me. "Can we entwine fingers?" Philip asked. "My mother taught me to do that with someone you have a lot in common with."

I smiled. I gave him my little finger. "I like you when you are not on your high horse," I said.

"I haven't gotten on a horse yet," said Philip. We pulled our pinkies apart.

"It's just an expression." I laughed.

At the last minute, Evan and Arthur showed up. "We want to go riding," they said to my father.

Philip whispered to me, "I thought perhaps we would have one day without the DeVaugns."

Arthur and Evan stared at us. "I wonder if they know that your mother was a champion horseback rider," I said to Philip.

"Everyone in Borgunlund knew about my mother and horses," said Philip, once again sounding a little snobby.

I looked at Philip holding on so tightly to his mother's saddle. That's when I noticed. There was a little zipper pocket in the leather of Philip's gorgeous saddle. And it was bulging. I wondered what was in it.

CHAPTER TWELVE

THE HORSE IN THE WAVES

Two open-air jeeps drove us to the stables on San Aurelia that were just inland from the beach. Lisette, the woman who runs the stable, was grooming a horse I had never seen before—a beautiful roan gelding with four white stockings, a high arch to his neck, and a slimmed-down look to his rump.

I jumped off the jeep and greeted Lisette with a hug. I had known her since I was a little girl. I introduced her to Philip. "Who's the new horse?" I asked Lisette.

"His name is Sir Gawain. He's a little high-strung. He's the most expensive piece of horseflesh we've got.

He's a retired racehorse and a good companion for Sir Galahad. Philippa, hold his head, will you?" Lisette asked. "I want to check his shoe."

She lifted the horse's leg and held it as if it weighed nothing, but I could see him shift his weight. "Move over!" said Philip to the horse, shoving it aside with his shoulder and helping Lisette.

"Thanks," said Lisette. "I can see that you've spent time around horses." She nodded in approval. Sir Gawain nudged my shoulder with his muzzle. He had beautiful soft brown eyes that looked clear and wide awake.

"He's really beautiful!" exclaimed Philip. "May I ride him?"

"I don't know. Exactly how much have you ridden?" Lisette asked.

"His mother rode in the Olympics," I told Lisette.

"That's his mother," said Lisette. "That doesn't mean he can ride. Why don't you start up on Dandelion?"

Philip looked at Dandelion with her big round belly. "No," he said defiantly. "I would like to ride the new horse. I am an excellent rider."

Lisette sighed. "Okay, go to talk to Philippa's father."

Dad always has riders do a preliminary easy ride around the rink first so he can get a good sense of who is lying about what good riders they are. Arthur and Evan were much better than I thought. I wondered about them. They were karate experts, horseback riders . . . and they were always around Philip. I wasn't sure what it all added up to, but I hoped that I had the patience to find out.

"Just let me see you go around the rink on Dandelion," Dad said to Philip.

Philip swung up on Dandelion's saddle. Philip got her to move in a faster trot than I had ever seen her move. He made Dandelion shift swiftly into a canter, keeping the lead on the inside leg. Then he made her switch leads. If he had been in a show, he would have gotten ten points for that one movement. It was clear that he wasn't lying when he said he was an expert. He had one of the best seats I had ever seen.

Dad and I nodded at each other. Philip had made us believers. "Okay," said Dad. "Lisette, you can saddle the new horse for Philip."

"I will do it," said Philip. "I have my own saddle."

Dad smiled. "Well, clearly, you know your way around horses. Why don't you and Philippa take Evan and Arthur with you? They look very comfortable in the saddle. We'll be right behind you, with the rest of the crowd. Just don't get too far ahead of us."

I picked up Philip's saddle for him. I decided now was a good time to ask about the lumpy thing in the little zipper pocket. "What's in here?" I asked. "Your mother's gold medal?"

Philip turned pale. "Give me that," he said. It was more like a command than a request. "Please," he finally added.

I handed him the saddle.

His horse sucked air into his stomach, trying to trick Philip into leaving the girth loose.

Philip waited until Sir Gawain exhaled and then pulled the girth tight. "You don't look like someone who saddles your own horses," I said to him.

Philip smiled at me. "My mother taught me that anyone who is around horses should know how to saddle his own horse," he said.

I checked the girth just to make sure that he had done it right. It was nice and tight.

Arthur and Evan sat on a bale of hay staring at us. They both let Lisette saddle their horses for them.

"Can't you do it faster?" complained Arthur.

Philip rolled his eyes. "I'm finished here," he said. "Let's go help."

We both walked over to help my father and Lisette saddle up the other horses.

Out of the corner of my eye, I saw Arthur and Evan go over to our horses, Sir Galahad and Sir Gawain. They started to mount them.

"Hey!" I shouted. "These aren't your horses."

"We like yours better," shouted Evan.

Philip picked up his riding crop.

"You will ride the horses you were assigned to," he said.

Arthur and his brother walked away from our horses, giving us dirty looks.

"Take it easy," I warned. "Remember, they are paying guests."

"I'll remember," said Philip.

We helped Arthur and Evan up onto the saddle of the horses my father had assigned to them. Arthur gave me another nasty look as he put his dirty boot in my hand and I gave him a boost onto his saddle.

I went over to Sir Galahad. I checked the girth on Sir Galahad and swung myself up. It's always a shock to mount a tall horse. The ground seems an immense distance away. I adjusted the stirrups and looked back at Philip. He was up in his saddle. We trotted over to where Dad was with Evan and Arthur and some of the other guests.

Philip's horse made little jumping motions side to side. Sir Galahad joined him. Their energy seemed to be catching. They were just more high-spirited than the other horses, and they wanted to run.

"Philippa," said Dad, "I am going to take my group along the marsh trail to the beach. Arthur and Evan are so much better than the others, they'll be bored just walking ... and so will Philip. You take the dune trail, at a slow canter, and we'll meet up on the beach."

Dad and I often split the groups up like this when there are riders of different levels.

I signaled for Philip and Arthur and Evan. Evan and Arthur were both slumped in their saddles and whispering together.

Our horses pranced impatiently as we stepped out of the protected dune grasses onto the beach. Philip grinned at me. "Come on," he shouted.

He clucked into his horse's ear and took off. I put a little pressure on Sir Galahad's flank. He swung into a canter. Up ahead of me, Philip's horse went into a canter, too.

Philip and I were riding side by side—the water splashing on our horses' legs. Without the protection of the trees, the wind ripped through my hair. I felt so happy. All week long, I had had to be so careful never to do anything wrong, always thinking about the duchess and her nephews and trying to figure out what was really going on with Philip.

Now I just let my mind go. Philip and I were both named for a lover of horses. We were living up to our names, cantering calmly at the edge of the sea—life didn't get much better than this!

I turned around to check on Arthur and Evan.

They were both kicking their horses hard! Instead of riding in a controlled canter, they came galloping up and overtook us.

Suddenly, I saw Arthur lift his riding crop. Philip's horse reared. The saddle began to slip and Philip was slowing slipping into the sea with it.

Then his saddle came off his horse. Philip grabbed for it, just as a wave came and swept him up. His horse reared onto his back legs, kicking out.

"Watch out!" I yelled. I urged my horse through the water. I grabbed for Philip and got hold of his wrist. He was heavy, and his foot was caught in the stirrup. I leaned back in the saddle and pulled on the reins. I pulled back again, hoping against hope that poor Sir Gawain would get my signal and not panic and back up.

Philip used his own body weight and the momentum of the wave to swing up behind me on my saddle.

Philip's horse had righted himself and shook himself out at the edge of the ocean. I grabbed his rein, and Philip was holding on tight to my waist. Our horses were lathered, and we were both soaking wet.

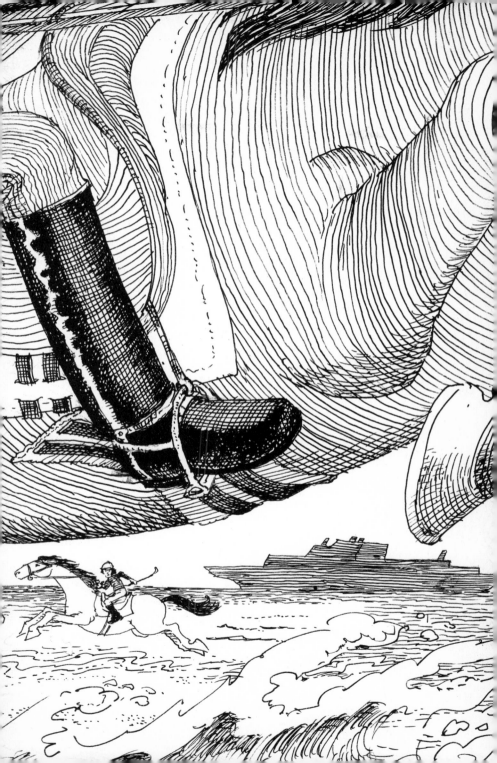

Arthur and Evan kept their horses on the beach several yards away from us. They made no attempt to help me, and because they were several yards away I couldn't read their expressions. But I had a feeling that they were not at all pleased that I had managed to rescue both Philip and his saddle. But why had they wanted Philip to fall, and why had they wanted the saddle?

I saw my father leading the other group. He came trotting up to us.

"What happened?" he demanded.

"I don't know," I admitted. "We were riding along, and then Arthur and Evan started to gallop by, and Philip fell off."

"I did not fall off," said Philip. "My saddle suddenly became loose." I turned to look at him. Only then did I see that there was a scratch on Philip's head. He was bleeding.

"You're hurt," I said.

"It's nothing," said Philip.

"Dad," I said, "I don't think it was an accident. I think Arthur raised his crop to make Philip's horse rear."

My father took command. "We're all going back to the stable," he announced to the group. "Slowly, at a walk. Are you all right, Philip?"

Philip wiped his head. His hand came away bloody. "I'm okay," he said. "It doesn't really hurt."

As soon as we got to the stables, Dad ordered Arthur and Evan to dismount. "Lisette," he said, "make sure these two stay here."

Dad took Philip into the first-aid room. I slipped off my horse and joined them.

"I'm fine," said Philip. "It's just a scratch. It's nothing."

"It's not very deep," said my father. "Scalp wounds do bleed a lot." Dad applied the antibiotic cream. "What happened?"

"My horse must have kicked up a rock," said Philip.

"That couldn't have happened," I said. "We were in the sand. There were no rocks. We were cantering in the waves, and suddenly the two DeVaugn boys took off at a gallop and shot past us," I said to Dad. "It looked as if Arthur raised his crop, and then Philip's saddle started slipping. There aren't rocks at the beach where Philip fell. How did he get that cut?"

"Maybe my horse's hoof hit me," said Philip.

Dad looked at Philip's wound again. "If that were true, I'd think it'd be deeper."

Dad touched the wound on Philip's head with another antiseptic pad. Philip shook his head. "Ouch," he said, "that hurts a little."

Just then Lisette came into the stable. She was carrying Philip's saddle and saddlebag. "I know I was supposed to stay put, but there's something I have to show you." She dropped the saddle down on some hay.

"This is the saddle that was on the boy's horse." She showed us the cinch. It was a clean cut. "It would never have come loose like that if someone hadn't cut it with a knife."

"Arthur or Evan," I said.

"I don't think so," said Philip. "I must not have checked the cinch."

"But you did," I said. "I did, too. Something happened when Arthur and Evan tried to mount our horses after we saddled them. And I think that they wanted you to fall off so they could get your saddle."

Philip grabbed his saddle from Lisette. He looked at

my father. "Your daughter's imagination is running away with her, just like my horse." He laughed. But I didn't think he was funny.

"Dad, I helped Philip saddle up his horse. It's a beautiful saddle. There wasn't a cut in the cinch before we rode out."

Dad stood up. "That's it," said my father. "We are going back to the ship."

"No," said Philip.

"Yes," said my father. "Your father may be in charge of the ship, but right now, you are not in charge. I am."

CHAPTER THIRTEEN
CHECKMATE

Dad went back to the group that was riding around the rink. "Excuse me, ladies and gentlemen," he said. "I'm afraid we have to return to the ship immediately. I know it's a disappointment, but I will arrange for a complimentary day at the spa with full body massages for everyone."

I heard Dad get on his cell phone and call the spa and explain to them what was going to happen. The staff on the ship was used to things happening on shore that required last-minute adjustments—sudden thunderstorms, a guide who doesn't show up, a bus that breaks down.

Dad took the saddle from Philip and examined it for himself.

"Please, sir," said Philip, "there's no reason why everyone has to go back to the ship. I can wait. Just give me back my saddle."

Dad shook his head. "We are all going back to the ship. Everyone will enjoy a massage." Dad's voice sounded cheerful and calm, but I know my dad. When he's nervous, he gets this false cheer in his voice. He was worried. And the truth was that I was, too. It had been scary when I saw Philip's horse rear in the ocean. I knew it wasn't an accident, and it wasn't my imagination.

The trip back to the ship was uneventful. Someone from the spa was waiting at the ship's tender dock with champagne for the guests. Most of them seemed perfectly happy with the change in plans.

My father told Philip and me to wait while he notified the captain that he wanted to speak to him. Philip and I sat by one of the swivel chairs on the game deck with a game of chess between us.

"I bet you play chess well," I said to Philip quietly.

"How do you know that?" he asked.

"This entire voyage has been like a chess game! Philip, you start to trust me, but you don't tell me the whole story. You know more about what's going on than you will tell me. You think you're three moves ahead of me. Arthur did something to your saddle, and you know it. It wasn't an accident that you fell."

"No, it wasn't," Philip admitted.

"And the crest on Evan's jacket was from Borgunlund!" I said. "They were pretending to be from the royal family of Borgunlund and you knew it. Now tell me how you knew."

"I knew that you were close to finding out everything about me," said Philip. "Believe me, my father and I have reasons why we don't want everyone to know."

"Does it have to do with the Borgunlund diamonds?" I asked.

"Yes," said Philip. "I told my father that you were too good a detective and that you would find out."

"What do the Borgunlund diamonds have to do with you?"

Philip looked down at the chess pieces. "My mother

was rumored to have the jewels hidden somewhere when she was killed."

"Killed? You told me that she was dead, but you never said she was killed."

"It was made to look like a car accident. It happened just six months ago. Neither my father nor I believe it was an accident. My father wanted to keep me close to him. He decided to take a job on a passenger cruise ship because he wasn't allowed to bring his son along in the navy. We thought I'd be safer here."

"You think your mother was killed?" I said. "How terrible! Why?"

"She was the Royal Princess of Borgunlund," said Philip. He had tears in his eyes. "Remember when I said you danced like a princess, just like my mother. But she really was a princess."

"And what about the diamonds?" I asked. "You mean there are real diamonds that the DeVaugns are looking for?"

Philip nodded. "We never found all of my mother's diamonds. My father and I thought they were in her mechanical birds, but we took them apart, and they

weren't in there. Then we thought they might be in Max's collar. I think the duchess thought so, too."

"I checked them. They were fake . . . ."

"Yes, the ones on Max's collar are definitely fake."

I started to think—hard. "Philip, you and your father gave Max that silly rhinestone collar in the hopes that it would tempt the jewel thieves after your mother's diamonds. You knew someone would think that the ones on Max were real—they were a trap to fool any potential jewel thieves."

Philip nodded. "I knew you would figure it out," he said.

I stared at the chess set and then back at him. "Havapoo, a mixture of Havanese and poodle. And Maximillian is a poodle from Borgunlund. The Duchess DeVaugn planned this whole voyage to get the jewels from your country. That's why she brought her dog . . . ."

"That's what I think, too," said Philip. He looked up. The captain and my father and mother were coming toward us. Dad was carrying the saddle.

"Papa," said Philip, "we have to trust Philippa and

her family and tell them what is going on. Philippa figured out most of it on her own."

"I don't think we should talk about it in a public space," said the captain. He held his hand out to me. "Come to my quarters. It will be easier to explain there. Trust me."

I looked at Philip. Those were the words that I had once said to him.

"Please," said Philip quietly.

I nodded. Mom, Dad, and I followed them into the captain's quarters.

CHAPTER FOURTEEN
DON'T CALL HER A DUCHESS

To my shock, the captain's quarters were crowded. The duchess was there with Evan and Arthur. One of the security guards was standing over them.

The duchess looked angry. "Captain," she said, "I demand an explanation. My poor, poor nephews went to enjoy a horseback ride, and they said all because of a silly accident they had to cut their ride short ... and this man"—she pointed at my father—"he behaved very rudely toward my poor nephews."

My father looked as if he were about to throttle her "poor nephews."

"It wasn't an accident," said the captain. "Philippa and her father saved my son's life. I asked you all here because I wanted to thank them."

"*Thank* them!" said the duchess. "You will want to throw the whole family off the ship when you realize what a mistake you've made."

The captain glared at her. "The Bath family is not going anywhere. Madame, it is you who will be escorted off the ship by the police. Philippa, your instincts were right. The duchess here is not just a con person. She is a renowned jewel thief, and she knew that my son inherited the famous jewels of Borgunlund. They are seven beautiful matching diamonds. For centuries, thieves have tried to get hold of them."

"And we came close," snarled the duchess.

"Perhaps," said the captain, "but not close enough. The six that we have found are safe in a Swiss bank. There was one that was missing, however."

"It wasn't in the dog collar. That one is fake," I said.

"We know," said the captain. "But the duchess didn't know it. Because my wife was famous for her love of animals, it made sense that the jewels would be hidden

among her many pets, either in her collection of mechanical birds or as an accessory for her beloved poodles. Once it became clear that the duchess was overly interested in my family, I had the security guards keep a close watch on her."

"I did nothing," said the duchess. "You said yourself that the jewels in the collar around your dog's neck are fake."

"Yes," said the captain, "I knew they were fake, but when Philip decided to go riding, you told your nephews to search the inherited saddle. I must give you credit. Neither Philip nor I thought about searching the saddle."

"Philippa figured it out, Papa," said Philip. "She was the one who noticed the bulge in the saddle. But when I went to look into it, Arthur saw me. That's why he tried to make me fall off my horse so he could get into the saddle."

I stared at Evan and Arthur. "I still haven't figured out something. Why did you rip off the crest of Borgunlund from your jacket?"

"My aunt's idea was stupid," snarled Arthur. "She

made up those phony crests. She thought it would help us get closer to Philip. But you seemed to be taking too much of an interest in us right from the get-go. Even that first day when you came over with ginger ale, I knew you were suspicious of us."

"Actually I was just trying to be nice then," I said. "I didn't get suspicious until you and your aunt started to show so much interest in me."

"Shut your mouth, Evan," said the duchess.

"Look, this was your idea to begin with," said Evan. He turned back toward us. "She told us that she'd take us on a free cruise if we just helped her. She said it would be like taking candy from a baby. Some baby!"

"I have arranged for Interpol to escort the duchess and the two of you off the ship," said the captain as he turned to the two boys. "I'm sure the authorities will be willing to be lenient with you if you tell them everything you know."

"We would have taken the diamond from the saddle if you hadn't been in the way," Arthur snarled at me.

"But you didn't," I said.

"Kiem *say!*" shouted Don Quixote.

"What is he saying?" Arthur demanded.

"Keep 'em safe!" I told him. "The parrot is protecting Philip. So is Maximillian and so am I. You didn't stand a chance."

"You and that lousy menagerie," snarled Arthur. "We should have sent them all overboard."

I looked up at the captain. "What about Lady Windermere? She belongs to the duchess! And she won't be able to take care of a dog if she's in jail."

"Don't call her a duchess," said the captain.

"Well, whoever she is—if she's in jail, who's going to take care of Lady Windermere?"

"I don't want her," snarled the duchess. "I don't care what happens to her. She was just a stray I picked up. I needed an excuse to get close to the royal dog of Borgunlund. She practically pooped in my handbag! You can throw her overboard for all I care."

"She's not going overboard," I said. "And she's not going with you."

I looked at my parents. Mom sighed. "Philippa, the crew is not allowed to have pets. You know that. The kennels are just for the passengers, and they pay a fortune for the privilege of bringing a dog on a cruise."

"Philip has Maximillian," I said.

The captain smiled down at me. "I think it would be unfair for my son to have a dog when you cannot. We can make an exception in this case. After all, the dog fell into your arms, so to speak."

"Thank you, Captain," I said.

I looked at Philip. "Let's go tell Lady Windermere."

The captain nodded. "I think you both can go now," he said. Once again, it was that captain's voice—but I was beginning to like it. Captain Raynor was right. The new captain was a good man.

"I want to thank you Philippa," said Captain Vittiganen. "You have been a good friend to my son and to me."

I almost felt like curtsying.

CHAPTER FIFTEEN

DON'T YOU THINK IT'S TIME YOU TRUSTED ME?

I went to the kennel. Little Lady Windermere was ecstatic to see me. Maximillian got up calmly.

I looked down at the floor. Lady Windermere had had another accident. Philip surprised me. "I'll clean it up," he said.

"Well, that's not something you see every day," I said. "A prince picking up poop."

Philip grinned at me.

We walked out onto the deck. "'Keep 'em safe,'" said Philip. "You even figured that out. Don Quixote was taught English by my mother. That was his warning call."

"I'm sorry your mother was in such danger," I said. "I wish I could have met her."

"My mother got Don Quixote when she was about the same age as we are now. She was at boarding school in England. I told you my mother would have liked you. She would have been glad that you are my friend."

Philip and I walked together with our dogs on the deck.

I looked at him. "You still haven't told me the whole truth, have you?" I said.

Philip looked at the shuffleboard numbers on the deck.

"Don't you think it's time you trusted me?" I said.

"My family background is difficult," said Philip slowly. "I haven't lied to you. My mother was an Olympic horsewoman. I was originally of royal blood. There was a revolution in my country. My mother was killed. And, yes, there are some people who do not wish my family well."

"So it wasn't just about the jewels, was it?" I said.

Philip shook his head. "The jewels were important . . . and they are worth a lot of money but, no, I do not think the people who hired the duchess wanted only the jewels."

Philip sighed. "I will understand if you want to keep your distance from me . . . . It might be safer."

He stroked Maximillian.

"You're my friend," I said.

Max gave me his paw. I shook it. He wanted some attention. "Did your mother give you Max to protect you?" I asked.

Philip shook his head. "No, she just loved poodles."

Little Lady Windermere was wagging her tail. "Well, now you have a Havapoo and me. We'll keep you safe," I said.

Philip grinned at me. "You know," he said, "I do feel safe with you . . . ." Philip turned to me. "I asked my father if I could show you something," he said.

"The royal crest of Borgunlund?" I asked.

"No," said Philip. "It's a little more valuable than that."

He reached into his pocket and pulled out a stone almost as big as my knuckle. It gleamed in the sunlight.

"You're kidding!" I gasped. "That's not the real diamond, is it?"

Philip nodded.

"Your father let you just put it in your pocket!"

"Well, technically it does belong to me, and I promised him I would bring it back and let him put it in the safe. But I wanted to show it to you. In a way, you were the one who found it. I never thought to look in my mother's saddle."

I moved away from the railing. The last thing I wanted to do was to bump Philip's arm and send the diamond into the bottom of the sea.

Philip followed me to a corner of the deck.

He held it out to me. "Go on," he said, "it's not going to bite you. You can hold it."

Gingerly I took it in both hands. It gleamed.

I breathed on it. For a second, there was a fog around the diamond, and then in an instant it cleared up.

Philip nodded. "You act as if you've been around

diamonds all your life," he said.

"No," I said. "That's your life—not mine."

"Well, diamonds are forever," said Philip.

"So are friends," I added.